First published in 2016 by Child's Play (International) Ltd
Ashworth Road, Bridgemead, Swindon SN5 7YD, UK

Published in USA by Child's Play Inc
250 Minot Avenue, Auburn, Maine 04210

Distributed in Australia by Child's Play Australia Pty Ltd
Unit 10/20 Narabang Way, Belrose, Sydney, NSW 2085

ISBN 978-1-84643-696-3
CLP090915CPL11166963

Printed in Shenzhen, China

1 3 5 7 9 10 8 6 4 2

A catalogue record of this book
is available from the British Library

www.childs-play.com

And then...

ALBOROZO

Oh, Brother...
As in MY brother.
He gets all the attention!
Even though it's MY birthday!

Humph.

Hey everybody!
Look at me!
Look at MY drawing!

And listen! I've got a story to tell you!

Once upon a time there was a baby brother who cried and cried and cried and nobody paid any attention to his big sister, okay? Babies are so annoying! They cry and smell and get slimy stuff all over their big sister's toys like a squid and nobody seems to mind because they can't help it... Anyway, the big sister made a special birthday wish! **AND THEN...**

Mom and Dad were so tiny they got chased by a huge bee even though it was

normal bee sized. They had to hide under a cupboard so the bee got bored and flew away to find honey for its dinner! AND THEN...

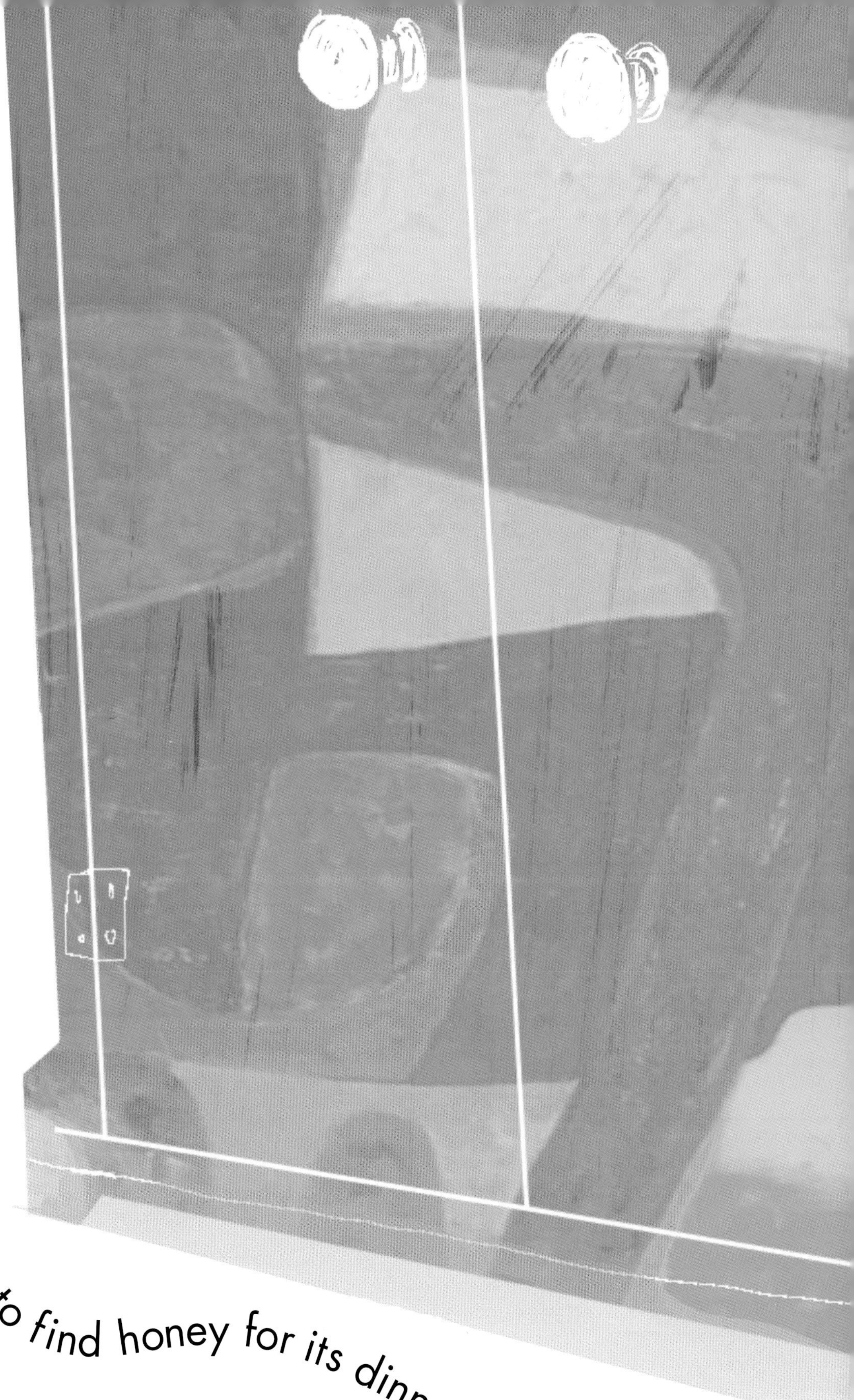

The baby brother squid was crying he was so hungry, but Mom was too tiny to feed

him so the big sister looked in the cupboard for squid food but there were only old crackers which were no good because they were too salty!

AND THEN...

The big sister heard a lot of crashing sounds and horrible wet slimy sounds so she ran into the living room and the baby brothe

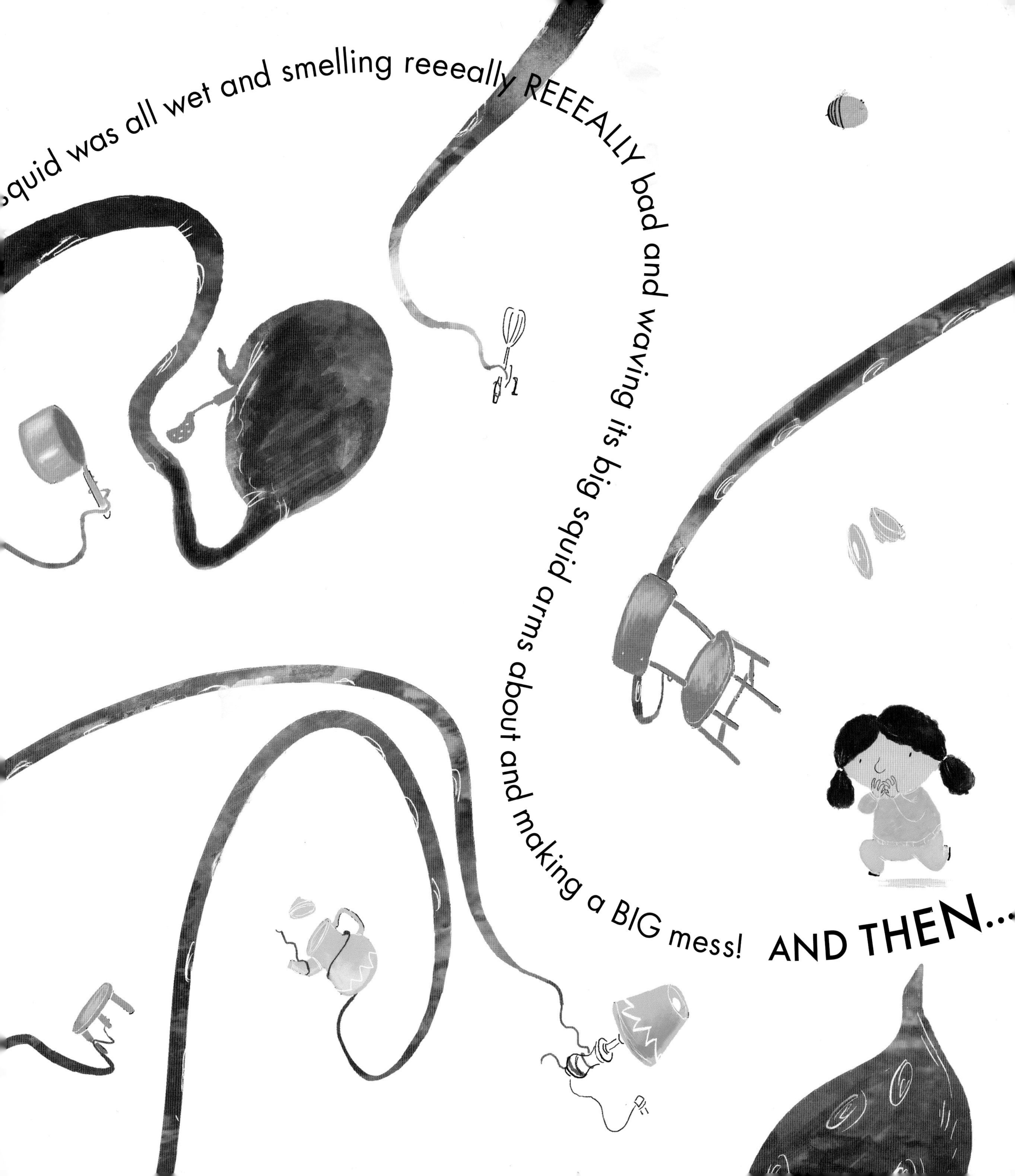
squid was all wet and smelling reeeally REEEALLY bad and waving its big squid arms about and making a BIG mess!
AND THEN...

The big *sister* was really clever and knew a squid doctor lived next door so she called the squid doctor on the telephone. (The big sister knew she could use the

telephone in an emergency so she called the squid doctor). AND THEN...

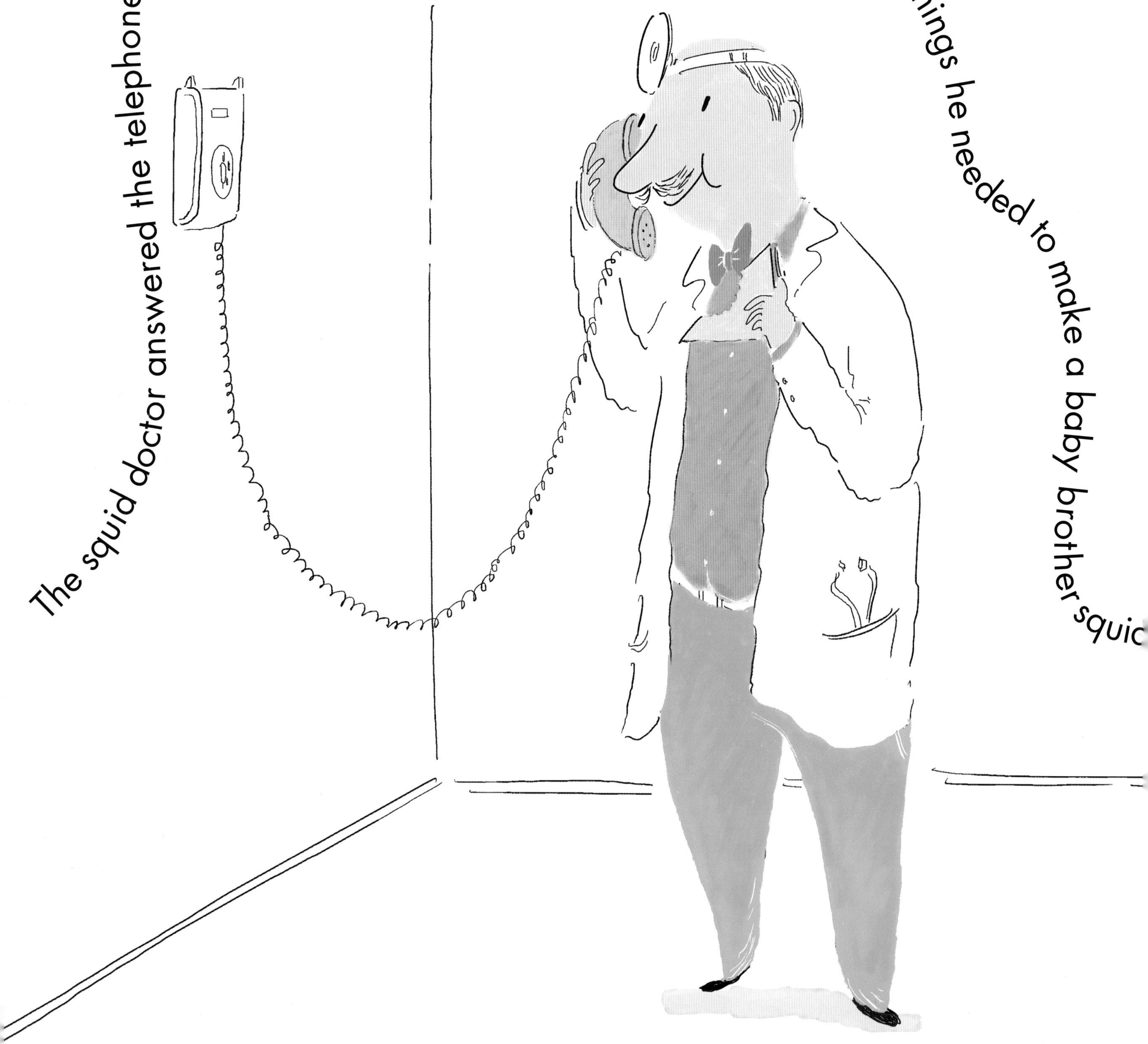

The squid doctor answered the telephone and was really happy because he had just bought all the things he needed to make a baby brother squic

better and he said he'd be right over even though he'd just made a sandwich. **AND THEN...**

The squid doctor knocked on the door and the big sister asked to see his iden-ti-fi-kay-shun just in case he was a stranger pretending

to be a squid doctor but he definitely was one so she let him in. **AND THEN...**

The squid doctor checked him over and said he needed special squid food

but he didn't know what it was because he had a tummy ache in doctor school that day so he missed that lesson. AND THEN...

The big sister knew who would know what the baby brother squid ate. MOM and DAD! So she ran into the kitchen

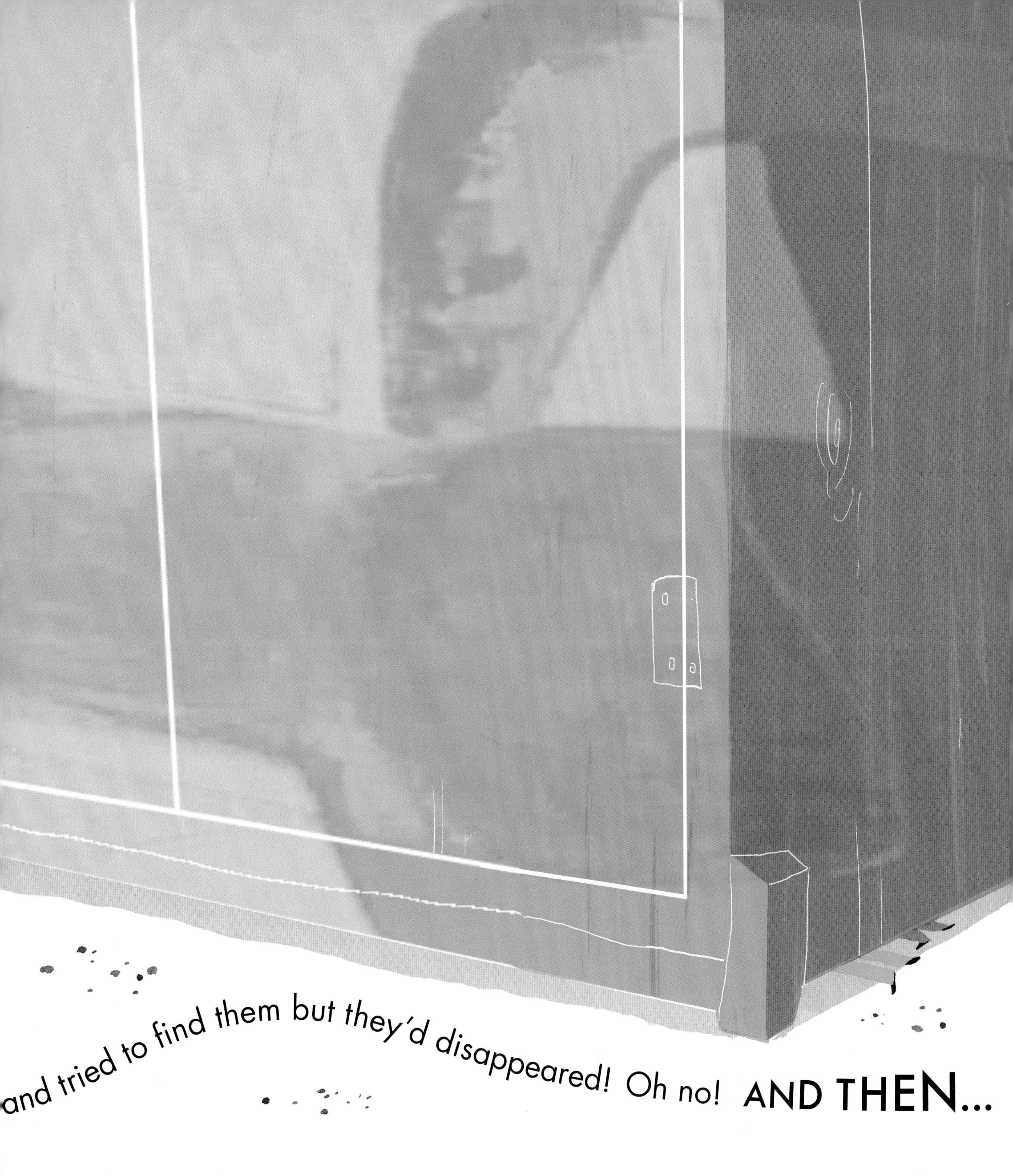

and tried to find them but they'd disappeared! Oh no! **AND THEN...**

The squid doctor put on his special glasses that let him see really tiny things and he found Mom and Dad sitting on half a cookie which Dad had promised to pick up last week but

hadn't but that was good because they had something to eat while they were hiding! **AND THEN...**

The big sister screwed her eyes up all tight and tried to make another wish.

which she was sure she could have as it was still her birthday and it was an emergency and she was getting scared. So she wished as hard as she could that her Mom and Dad were big again and that her baby brother wasn't a giant slimy squid anymore but her real baby brother who wasn't that bad I suppose as long as he left her toys alone.

AND THEN...

Wait, everybody!

That's my baby brother crying!

He's NOT such a stinky, slimy squid anymore!

He's quite nice really.

Maybe he'd like to hear a story?

Once upon a time,
a big sister sat down with her baby brother,
who still smelt kind of funny, but not as bad as
when he was a squid, and he was smiling at her
and looking a bit cute, I suppose.

AND THEN...